PICKLE
&
PENGUIN

LAWRENCE DAVID

illustrated by
SCOTT NASH

Dutton Children's Books

NEW YORK

For Maya Janhavi David —L.D.

For David and Kim —S.N.

Library of Congress Cataloging-in-Publication Data

David, Lawrence.
Pickle and Penguin / by Lawrence David; illustrated by Scott Nash.—1st ed.
p. cm.
Summary: A talking pickle with a television show meets a penguin
in Antarctica and brings him back to New York City.
ISBN 0-525-47102-2
[1. Penguins—Fiction. 2. Pickles—Fiction. 3. New York (N.Y.)—Fiction]
I. Nash, Scott, ill. II. Title.
PZ7.D2823 Pi 2004
[Fic]—dc22 2003062483

Published in the United States by Dutton Children's Books,
a division of Penguin Young Readers Group
345 Hudson Street, New York, New York 10014
www.penguin.com

Manufactured in China
First Edition
1 3 5 7 9 10 8 6 4 2

Pickle was the only talking pickle in the world. He lived in New York City and had his own TV talk show. On his program, people told stories and did funny tricks. Sometimes Pickle even visited exciting places like Shanghai or a bowling alley.

When Pickle got home every night, he poured himself a glass of brine, then walked through his large apartment from the kitchen to the ballroom to the movie theater to the living room.

Pickle sat by the window and looked out at all the smiling, laughing people in their homes. He took off his necktie and slumped down in one of his fancy chairs. It wasn't easy being the world's only talking pickle.

One day for a special show, Pickle took a trip to Antarctica. When he got off the boat, he saw penguins swimming and eating, but they were all too busy to talk.

Then Pickle spotted one penguin standing alone.

"Anything wrong, fella?" he asked.

Penguin stared at the talking pickle. "You speak Penguinese?" Penguin asked.

Pickle nodded. "And Italian, French, Russian, and Kosher Dill. So why aren't you with your pals?"

"It's too cold here," Penguin said. "I need a change from all this fish and ice."

"Then why not go somewhere else?" Pickle asked.

Penguin put a wing to his head. "Somewhere else? I've never been *somewhere else* before."

Pickle laughed. "Well, then today's your lucky day—*I'm* from somewhere else. Come on along."

Pickle and Penguin stood on the boat's deck. The ship sailed up the coast of South America. The air grew warmer. Penguin hopped excitedly and pointed to the trees along the shore. "What are those green things?" he asked.

"Those are trees," Pickle said.

Penguin looked at Pickle. "You're green. Are you a tree?"

Pickle shook his head. "Not by a long shot, buddy. I'm a sour pickle."

As the ship entered New York Harbor, Penguin pointed to a large green lady standing in the water. "Is she a sour pickle or a tree?" he asked.

"She's the Statue of Liberty," Pickle told him. "She welcomes people to America."

"Will she welcome a penguin?" Penguin asked.

"Penguins, pickles, and people," Pickle said. "Everyone's welcome here. Lady Liberty shines her torch for those lost from all over the world."

Penguin and Pickle stepped into the city. Horns honked, signs flashed, and cars, buses, and people rushed in every direction. "Now make sure you stay with me," Pickle said. "Just hold my—"

"Look at that!" Penguin shouted. He pointed his wing at all the giant, sparkly icicles rising out of the ground. "How can those grow in such warm weather?"

Penguin ran across the street to touch one.

"Wait!" Pickle called.

But before he could follow his friend, a swarm of people crowded the sidewalk, and Penguin was nowhere to be seen.

"I think I've lost him," Pickle said, shaking his head.

Penguin ran down the street, poking the giant icicles. "None of them are cold," he said. "Why aren't they cold, Pickle?" He turned around to hear Pickle's answer, but Pickle wasn't there.

Penguin hopped up and down, looking around. All he saw

were towering icicles and lots of odd creatures hurrying in many directions. "I think I've lost him," he said, shaking his head. "Can anyone help me find my friend? I think I'm lost."

No one answered. No one seemed to know any Penguinese.

Penguin followed a group of odd creatures into one of the icicles, then into a box. The box moved up and then down, but Penguin didn't find Pickle.

Penguin followed some of the odd creatures into a hole, then into a long tube. The tube jostled about, but Penguin didn't find Pickle.

Penguin climbed out of the hole and found hundreds of little pickles in a tub. "Have you seen Pickle?" he asked. The little pickles didn't answer.

Penguin scratched his head and wondered what to do next. Then he remembered what Pickle had told him about the special lady who helped when you were lost.

While Penguin searched for Pickle, Pickle searched for Penguin. Pickle got into a helicopter, flew over the city, and looked out through his binoculars. But Pickle didn't find Penguin.

Pickle went to the top of the Empire State Building and hung a giant banner. PENGUIN I'M UP HERE! the sign read. But Pickle didn't find Penguin.

Pickle hopped into his limousine and drove up and down the streets with his head sticking out of the sunroof. But Pickle didn't find Penguin.

"Mr. Pickle, it's time to get to the studio for the show," his driver told him.

That's when Pickle got an idea. "Perfect," he declared. "Let's get a move on!"

Pickle rushed onstage for his show. The audience cheered.

"Hey there, folks," Pickle said. "Welcome to *The Pickle Show*.
My new friend is lost somewhere in the city." He held up pictures
of Penguin from their trip. "Penguin is a swell bird," Pickle said.
"He's friendly, funny, and curious. And I gotta admit, I do miss
this bird quite a bit. He almost makes me feel half-sour. So if you
see him, please give me a ring. Thanks."

At the same time, Penguin stepped off a ferryboat and onto the island where the giant green lady stood. Just as he was about to ask her for help, his stomach rumbled. "Oh my!" Penguin exclaimed. "I'd hate to talk to the green lady with a rumbly tummy. She'd think I was as rude as a sea lion."

He watched as a little odd creature spoke to a big odd creature with a shiny cart.

"Pretzel, please," the little creature said.

The big creature gave the little creature a curly thing. The little creature stuck it in her mouth, took a bite, and smiled.

Penguin waddled over to the big creature with the cart. "Pretzel, please," he said.

The big creature looked from his mini-TV to Penguin.
"Penguin!" he shouted. He reached for his cell phone.

Penguin gave the curly thing a peck. It was warm and delicious!
Much tastier than fish. He smiled at the giant green lady. "If you
help me find Pickle, I'll share my warm pretzel with you," he said
quietly. "I really would like to find my friend."

The green lady didn't answer.

"Maybe I need to get closer so she can hear me."

Penguin walked into a door at the bottom of the green lady.

After climbing stairs for a while, Penguin stopped. "Can you help me find Pickle?" he called out.

The green lady didn't answer.

"I guess she can't hear me yet," Penguin said, so he climbed higher.

Finally, he reached a spot where he couldn't go any farther. Penguin leaned out a window just above the giant green lady's ear. He held his pretzel out to her. "I saved you a big piece. Will you help me find Pickle?" he asked.

Before the lady could answer, Penguin heard a shout.

"Hey, friend, look this-a-way!"
Penguin turned—and saw Pickle!
"Hello!" Penguin shouted.

Penguin climbed aboard the flying boat and gave Pickle
a big hug.

He turned and tossed the last of the pretzel to the green lady.
"Thanks for finding Pickle!" he told her.
"She's a swell gal," Pickle said, laughing.

That evening, Pickle took Penguin on a tour of his apartment, showing him the kitchen, the ballroom, the movie theater, and the living room.

"You know, this city is an interesting place. I like it now that we're together," Penguin said. "And living in this tall, warm icicle is very nice."

Pickle and Penguin slumped down side by side in Pickle's fancy chairs and gazed out at the city. "Was it scary being lost in a strange place?" Pickle asked.

Penguin nodded. "I'd say so," he replied. "It's quite a big city."

"I understand," Pickle said. "But now you know that if you're ever lost, I'll always find you."

"Always?" Penguin asked.

"Always," Pickle replied.

Penguin smiled. "That's a good thing to know." His stomach rumbled loudly, and he covered it with a wing.

"Hungry for a snack?" Pickle asked his friend.

Penguin laughed. "Always," he said.